Christmas

on

Harmony Lane

Christmas

on

Harmony Lane

Drew Beyson

ISBN: 979-8-9939767-0-9 (paperback)

Contents

A Visit to Harmony Lane

ELAINE BAXTER PAUSED AFTER her long travel at the foot of the porch steps of her rental cottage. Her gloved hand still clutched her suitcase handle as a swirl of snowflakes welcomed her. A few gentle flakes drifted down from a low-hanging North Carolina sky, brushing against the brim of her hat like small whispers of welcome. The cottage for the next few months stood warm and bright against the early afternoon gray. Its green shutters, stone chimney, wreath of twigs, pinecones, and cranberry-red ribbon decorated the door. "Well," she murmured, her voice almost lost in the chill of the air. "This is a change."

After decades on the move, documenting vibrant corners of the world for travel magazines and photography journals, she hadn't stayed put for more than a season. Harmony Lane, with its cozy energy for her new retirement and promise of snow-dusted peace, felt like a strange stillness. But her sister Carol was right. It was time to rest, to reset, to see if she could belong somewhere again.

A bell tinkled as she opened the front door, and it creaked as it opened. She loved the sound, as it gave her a sense of security. The cottage smelled of cedar and faint lemon polish, a welcome contrast to the stale airport terminal she'd left that morning and hotel rooms. She had packed boxes that arrived ahead of her, which her sister stacked in the corner. Her loom and fabrics held a lifetime of stories folded into cloth.

Carol stopped by within the hour, arms full of groceries and unsolicited enthusiasm. "I still can't believe you did it," Carol said as she unpacked cheese, crackers, Earl Grey, English Breakfast teas, and the rest of the groceries. "Elaine Baxter, international woman of mystery, lands."

"I didn't land," Elaine said, sliding a box cutter across a stack of labeled cardboard. "I circled low and figured I'd give Harmony Lane a test run."

They laughed, falling into an easy rhythm as only sisters could. Carol, five years younger and settled in a neighboring town, had been trying to lure Elaine to the area for over a year. "You need a place that inspires you and lets you breathe," she'd said more than once.

Elaine wasn't convinced she needed anything, but breathing room sounded nice.

Later that afternoon, Carol presented her with a flyer from the local community board, excited that she would take part.
"Don't say no yet," she warned.

Elaine did a quick read of the flyer, the page crinkling as she glanced over the words. Then she read it aloud: "'Harmony Lane Annual Indoor Christmas Art & Music Exhibit. Calling all creators, performers, and appreciators!' Really, Carol?"

"Do it," Carol encouraged. "You could show your textiles. Your weaves are stunning, and this town eats up anything with a story behind it. And your stories are captivating."

Elaine raised an eyebrow. "I'm not a performer."

"It's not just music. It's art too," Carol added. "Locals sell everything from hand-painted cards to quilts to jewelry. There's even an open mic this year."

"I can promise you this: I will not be open mic-ing anything," Elaine quipped with a whimsical look.

Carol grinned and handed her a pen. "Sign up anyway. It's the best way to meet people around here. Besides... don't you want your work seen?"

Elaine hesitated, the flyer still in her hand. Perhaps she did. Maybe she wanted something else, too: connection, warmth, a little magic. Christmas had a way of stirring up old wishes, even the ones you'd shelved.

That evening, she walked the few blocks to check out the exhibit's sign-up location. Homes with twinkling lights, wreaths on their doors, and Christmas trees lit and visible through the window reminded her of old-time Christmases, bringing a smile as she neared the shop. Arriving at the English ivy-wrapped storefront with old-style gold lettering across the window that read Melody's Vintage Music & Arts, she stepped inside. A warm light spilled across shelves of sheet music, dusty instruments, and a counter with a bell she tapped. After taking a breath, with a laugh, she wondered if that was what music smelled like.

An older man emerged from the back, tall, gray-haired, dressed in a flannel shirt and jeans that suggested practical use, not fashion. His expression was polite, a little guarded. "Help you with something?"

Elaine offered her hand. "I'm here to sign up for the exhibit. I was told this was the place."

He nodded once, then walked behind the counter, pulling out a clipboard. "Tom Callahan. I'm... hosting the event this year." He didn't elaborate.

As she leaned forward to fill out the form, her tote caught the edge of a precarious stack of sheet music. It toppled, the pages fluttering as if in slow motion, with a gentle thud and a bell-like jingle.

She froze as their eyes met. "Oh no. I'm so sorry."

Tom raised an eyebrow and crouched to gather the mess. "Well, I guess we've got our newest performer."

Elaine kneeled to help. "Only if there's a prize for best accidental percussion."

Tom cracked a smile as he straightened, holding the last of the sheet music in his hand. "I think I've got the trophy for that one locked up. Years of stacking these too high with too little support, as we've found out."

Elaine smiled, sensing the crack in his otherwise solid, stoic shell. "Then I'll accept honorable mention and a strong cup of coffee."

He didn't laugh, but his expression softened. He nodded toward the clipboard. "If you still want to sign up, I'll need your name and what you're planning to show or perform."

She grabbed the pen and signed up. "Elaine Baxter. Textiles. Hand-woven pieces, mostly with natural dyes. A mix of tradition and travel, I suppose."

Tom looked at her again, this time with more curiosity in his eyes. "Travel?"

She nodded. "Retired photographer. I spent the last couple of decades living out of a suitcase and taking pictures for magazines and nonprofits. Now I stitch stories instead of snapping them. While I was traveling, stitching filled those quiet times."

He let out a low whistle. "Can't say I've ever met anyone who's stitched stories."

"Well," she said, tucking a stray curl behind her ear, "stick around. I just might convert you."

A beat passed between them. Pleasant, but unspoken, before she finished filling out the form and slid the clipboard and pen back across the counter. "I'm told this is a great way to meet people," she said. "Community spirit and all that."

Tom gave a small shrug. "That's what they tell me, too."

"You don't believe it?"

"I believe it... just never tested it for myself." He set the clipboard aside and walked around to the other side of the counter. "I kept to the road until taking over the store after my father's recent death. First holiday season standing still in a long time. I guess we have something in common, living on the road, so to speak."

Elaine could relate as her curiosity piqued. "Well, maybe standing still isn't so bad. It's a new thing for me too. We could learn together!"

He gave her a thoughtful look. "We'll see."

The door chimed behind her as she stepped out into the cold evening air. Elaine lingered on the sidewalk outside the music shop longer than she intended, her breath curling into the air like questions that hadn't quite taken shape. Snowflakes landed on her coat sleeves and melted right away. Across the street, a storefront was decorated with hand-painted ornaments and knitted stockings. A shopkeeper inside waved at a bundled child who pressed mittened hands to the glass. It all felt so... earnest, bringing back earlier memories. She sensed there were secrets to uncover here.

A cafe with twinkling lights strung along its roofline caught her eye. The smell of nutmeg and espresso wafted through the door as a couple stepped out with to-go cups. On a whim, Elaine ducked in behind them.

It was warm inside, crowded in a cozy way. Locals sat by the windows and wherever they could find a seat, sipping their beverages and talking with the kind of familiarity she hadn't known in years. A chalkboard sign above the counter read: "Comfort in a Cup – Try our Cinnamon Cream Coffee!"

Comfort in a cup? I gotta have one of those, she thought. She went to the counter and ordered one, then found a small table near the front window and took a moment to let herself relax, dropping her shoulders. Her hands wrapped around the mug, absorbing the heat as her mind wandered back to her visit with Tom.

There was something about him that didn't feel awkward, but reserved. Someone who had learned to keep his most important parts of himself tucked deep, safe from casual inquiry. *He told me he had been on the road for a long time. After all, wasn't she doing the same thing?*

It was odd, in a lovely way, to be noticed by someone who didn't know her name ten minutes earlier, not because of her accomplishments or her travels. Okay, knocking over the sheet music helped make a memory. Yet he **noticed** her.

She took a sip of the coffee. Sweet, strong, spicy. *Comforting, as advertised, and it' is in a cup!*

A woman passed by the window, waving at someone inside. She wore a patchwork coat and carried a cello case on her back. A blooming artist, perhaps. Another story waiting to be told. Elaine found herself smiling.

This town pulsed with creative energy, not in a polished gallery way, but in a natural way that suggested everyone had something to contribute. Harmony Lane was living up to its name.

She finished enjoying her cinnamon cream coffee and then stepped out into the snowy evening, cheeks warm, spirits steadier than they'd been in a long time. *Maybe Carol was right. Maybe this was the season to stop observing life from behind the lens and start stitching herself into it.* The charm and curiosity of this place and its Christmas traditions were grabbing her attention.

By the time she reached her cottage, snow clung to the edges of her boots, and a hint of pine had settled in her hair. She paused at the threshold, just long enough to whisper, "Okay, Harmony Lane. Let's see what we've got."

Snow continued to fall, settling into the crooks of tree branches and the seams of parked cars. Lights glowed in windows up and down the street. Gold, warm, full of things she hadn't quite named yet. Once she got settled in her cottage, she set a kettle on the stove to enjoy some of that English Breakfast tea Carol brought over. She pulled a throw blanket around her shoulders. The home still felt unfamiliar, its corners too sharp, the air too quiet. But she noticed something promising in how her rugs brightened the floorboards, and her fabrics felt as if they belonged here. Like maybe she did too, as she wondered. Did she pick this cottage... *or did it pick her?*

She walked into the spare room, where boxes labeled "Studio" sat stacked and waiting. As her tea steeped, she opened the top box and lifted out a folded swath of cloth dyed in deep indigo and turmeric orange. It smelled of lavender and road dust.

She'd woven this piece during a six-week trip to Rajasthan, just before she retired. It had survived five airports, a monsoon, and the existential crisis of when she turned sixty-five. And now it was here, waiting for its second act. She ran her fingers across the warp and weft, smiling to herself. Perhaps this Christmas isn't about returning to something lost, but stepping into something new.

Spilling Music and Tea

After having breakfast, Elaine went out to walk around the town and stop by Melody's so she could plan her part of the exhibit.

The town evoked cherished memories for her as she took in the old-time holiday feel and peaceful surroundings on this beautiful day. There were children outside playing as their moms were looking out their windows.

She arrived at Melody's Vintage Music and Arts and stepped inside the shop.

The bell above the door jingled with its now familiar sound. Tom looked up from behind the counter, where he was wrestling with a ball of tangled extension cords and blinking string lights. His expression teetered somewhere between irritation and resignation.

"Good morning," Elaine said.

Tom gave a short nod. "You're back? Again?"

"I had such a thrilling time knocking over your sheet music collection yesterday, I thought I'd try it again."

A corner of Tom's mouth twitched, an eyebrow lifting in mock suspicion. "Let me hide the sheet music first."

She set her canvas tote on the counter. "Brought you something. Some pine sprigs to make this store feel more like Christmas, and some

Holiday Blend tea. Figured you might need something Christmasy besides black coffee to keep your spirits up while untangling that mess," pointing to the ball of Christmas lights.

Elaine leaned on the counter as he poured hot water into a chipped mug she hadn't noticed earlier. He fumbled with the teabag, like someone who didn't drink tea but knew enough to be polite.

"Did this place always smell like wood polish and old brass?" she asked, smiling as she glanced around.

"Probably. My dad had a thing for keeping everything as it was; it's how I have always remembered it smelling here." Tom held the mug toward her for inspection, as if checking whether he'd done it right.

She took a sip. "Strong, with a kick of citrus. A little bold, but surprisingly smooth. Like you in a cup."

Tom blinked at her, then coughed. "That's not going on the sign."

They both laughed, and a feeling of ease settled between them. He picked up a tangled clump of string lights and motioned toward a stool. "You want to help me sort these? I promise it's a little more fun than watching them blink like dying stars."

She accepted and took a clump of lights. "You ever think these lights have attitudes? Like they wait until you need them most and then decide to protest?"

"Sure do," he said, surprising her. "I think they unionize in the box over the summer."

Elaine grinned. "Solidarity among seasonal decor. I respect it."

As they worked side by side untangling the mess, their hands bumped. "Nothing lingered, but each accidental touch stirred an awareness neither of them had expected. Intimate without being flirtatious."

Tom raised an eyebrow as he accepted the tea with a nod. "Thanks. You didn't have to."

"I know. That's what makes it nice," Elaine replied, then glanced at the string of lights. "Do those even work?"

He clicked a plug into a wall socket. Half the strand blinked on, sputtering as if they were unsure about commitment. "They did. Last year. I might have you help me with these if they don't cooperate."

Elaine laughed. That could turn into quite an adventure. She then wandered further into the shop, pausing at a shelf stacked with old jazz records and well-worn music books. The room had a cozy, lived-in feel. Not messy, but lived-in, like the shop had grown into its space as much as the man who ran it. "So," she said, turning back to him. "How are you planning to set up the exhibit?"

Tom exhaled. "Honestly? I'm not sure yet. My dad used to handle that. He ran this shop for forty years and hosted the exhibit every December. He passed away in the spring."

Elaine softened. "I'm sorry."

Tom gave a small nod. "Thanks. He loved this place. I inherited it and figured I'd keep him and the tradition going, but I didn't get the playbook for how he did this."

"Well, lucky for you, I've planned pop-up galleries in places much stranger than this. Ever curated a mobile exhibit inside a retired double-decker bus in the Scottish Highlands?"

He blinked. "Can't say I have."

"It was a windy disaster, but a stunning one," she said, then smiled. "I'd be happy to help organize the exhibit here with you. Might be a good way for me to learn names and faces."

Tom hesitated, then nodded. "Alright. I could use some help. It's often locals who sign up, but the crowd's grown over the years. We move shelves around, set up small tables, and hang things on the walls. Usually a dozen artists, a few musicians."

Elaine set her tote beside the counter after she pulled out a small sketchbook. "Here's an idea. If we cluster similar mediums together, we can create small zones. Textiles near the front, where the light's best. Jewelry, and small crafts on the display table, and the back corner as a music nook. What do you think?"

Tom studied her sketch again, nodding. "You've really got an eye for this."

Elaine sat on the edge of an old piano bench. "When I photograph, I'm always asking, 'Where does the eye land first?' In fabric, I ask, 'Where does the hand want to touch?' But with curation, it's both. You want people to move through the space as if they're walking through a story."

"That's... poetic," Tom said, rubbing the back of his neck. "My dad used to say the shop told stories just by staying put."

Elaine smiled. "Then we're not changing it. Just letting it speak a little louder for a few days."

He looked around as if seeing the space for the first time. "This table could go under the front window for the natural light. And maybe we hang the photo prints near the door, so people linger there."

Elaine raised an eyebrow. "See, you're not bad at this either."

Tom shrugged. "I've watched enough Decembers happen in this room. I guess I know what doesn't work."

"Then between us, we've got what does."

The plan took shape in more than lines on paper. It expressed itself through tone, shared values, and an understanding of what it meant to care about how things felt, not just how they looked.

Tom studied the rough sketch. "Do you have those in your head?"

"Occupational hazard. I once had to design a pop-up exhibit in a jungle clearing with nothing but banana leaves and twine. This will be a breeze."

He chuckled a low, rusty sound that felt underused. "Alright, I'm impressed."

They worked together while she learned the creaks and noises the store made for a while. Tom was familiar with those sounds as he continued his work. Elaine paced the floor, measuring with her steps, while Tom unpacked a box of instruments his father had kept on top shelves: an old clarinet, a saxophone, even a dusty oboe case.

Elaine turned when she heard the click of the oboe latch. "You play?"

Tom shrugged. "Used to. Still do, sometimes. Just not in front of people."

"Why not?"

He looked at her, then down at the instrument. "Never felt like there was a point. Music was a way of keeping sane while on the road. Something for the cab when the miles got too long."

Elaine leaned against the counter. "Funny. We're not that different. My camera was my sanity. Framing the world made it feel manageable."

He nodded. "So now you weave it instead."

"Exactly. Cloth tells a story, just like music, from different perspectives. You can feel the rhythm in it, the tension, the flow. I think that's why I stuck with it."

Tom glanced down at the oboe in his hands. "Maybe that's why I never got rid of these."

Elaine stepped closer. "You know, the exhibit has an open music set. Just saying."

He scoffed. "I don't perform."

"Neither do I," she replied with a wink. "But here we are."

The shop fell quiet again, but something else had shifted. A thread pulled taut between them, not quite tugging, but present. Elaine picked up a small broom she found and began sweeping where boxes had left a trail of dust.

"You don't have to clean," Tom said, though he didn't stop her.

"I know. That's what makes a place nice," she echoed, throwing him a look over her shoulder.

He shook his head, but the smile stayed longer this time.

After the shop was tidied and the sketch finalized, Tom turned the 'Closed' sign around on the door. But he didn't want her to leave.

"Do you have a few more minutes?" he asked, not quite meeting her eye.

Elaine tilted her head. "I think I can spare a few."

He nodded toward the bench by the window, and she followed. The evening light had dimmed to a soft blue-gray, casting a hush over the shop. Outside, the snow was falling again, gentle, persistent.

Tom disappeared into the back room and returned with a small leather-bound book. He held it out. "This belonged to my dad. Notes about the shop, vendors, inventory, music pieces he wanted to restore. But toward the end, he began jotting down things he overheard from customers. Snippets of conversation, jokes, favorite songs."

Elaine accepted it with intrigue, as if it might still contain something Tom hadn't found yet. She flipped through a few pages. In neat handwriting, the notes read:

"Dottie says her husband sings like a dying crow, request: please no Elvis this year."

"Benny's grandson learned 'Silent Night' on the clarinet, might cry."

"Carol mentioned she had a sister, Elaine. A traveler. Intriguing."

She looked up, eyebrows raised.

Tom looked sheepish. "He was... observant."

"I'll say." Elaine closed the book with care. "This is a treasure."

He glanced around the room again. "Sometimes I wonder if I'm doing it justice. The shop, the exhibit... him."

Elaine set the book on the windowsill. "You are. You're not replicating his version. You're building your own, with pieces of his legacy stitched into it."

They sat there for a moment, letting the silence settle, watching the snow fall.

Elaine stood. "Tomorrow, same time?"

Tom turned toward her. "You're volunteering now?"

"Well, someone has to keep the lights from staging a rebellion."

He gave a soft laugh. "Alright then. Tomorrow. Looking forward to it."

He gave a small, grateful nod.

By the time she left that evening, the layout was sketched, the floor space was almost clear, and a fresh pot of Holiday Blend tea steeped beside the register. Elaine paused at the door, enjoying the smell of the tea filling the air.

She lingered outside the shop, feeling the cold and wind. The lights inside glowed through the front window. For a moment, she imagined what the space would look like once it was filled with music, color, and life. A curated chaos. A minor symphony of community.

As she stepped back out onto Harmony Lane, Elaine felt the subtle thrill of something beginning. There was a rhythm forming beneath the surface of her new life. A harmony, tentative but true.

She wasn't used to this part, being in the picture instead of taking it. Participating. Planning. Belonging.

The wind picked up as she walked, but she didn't shiver. Instead, she tucked her scarf closer and let herself imagine what might come next: a new pattern, a new rhythm, a new strand in the weave of her story. The homes along the street were still lit up. The sound of Christmas music broke through the wind and calm.

Back at the cottage after she finished dinner, she would jot down a few alternative layout notes in her sketchbook. Maybe even guess what kind of music Tom might play if no one was watching. And yet, as she moved through the hush of falling snow, she realized she wasn't chasing a new beginning:

She might already be standing in it.

Weaving Textiles and Reeds

THE NEXT MORNING, ELAINE arrived earlier than usual, bundled in a thick wool coat and wearing a plum-colored scarf she had woven herself last winter. A dusting of snow covered the sidewalk, crunching underfoot as she approached Melody's. Warm yellow light glowed through the front window. She paused a moment to admire the quiet promise of a new day.

The bell chimed as she stepped inside, and the familiar scent of aged wood and distant brass greeted her like an old memory. Tom was already there, wearing a faded gray hoodie and moving a stack of old music stands to the side wall. He looked up, surprised but not displeased.

"You're early," he said.

"You had the lights on. It felt like an invitation."

Elaine hung her coat near the door and took a breath, letting the familiar scent of the shop blend with the pine ground her. Each time she entered, it felt a little more like the rhythm of a new routine, the hum of the shop a balm for her restless spirit.

Tom nodded toward the kettle. "Tea's on. I'm learning."

She smiled as she stepped behind the counter to pour a cup. "Next thing I know, you'll be offering scones and linen napkins."

He scoffed. "Don't push your luck. But was that a hint?"

Elaine shook her head and carried her tea to the central table, where she'd spread out swatches of fabric, sketches, and a few miniature display stands. "I was thinking I could build up the space with a layered texture. Like a cozy corner you wander into at just the right time."

Tom paused in his stacking. "You mean like...a fort?"

She laughed. "A very elegant one. With curated lighting."

She imagined soft, hanging lights filtering through the fabric, casting gentle shadows that moved like the echoes of music across the walls.

He grinned and returned to moving the stands. "Can't argue with that."

They worked together for the next hour and had only one brief difference of opinion, which they worked through, regarding the layout for the booths. Elaine chose her booth space with care, laying down a pale blue table runner over a reclaimed wood table. On it, she arranged handwoven scarves, small quilted ornaments, and tiny framed fabric collages. Her style was quiet but rich with story, inviting touch as much as admiration.

Tom, meanwhile, tackled a forgotten corner of the shop. A small mountain of dusty instrument cases, music stands, and promotional signs leaned against the back wall. He opened a narrow storage closet, and Elaine heard him mutter something that sounded suspicious, like a plea to the universe.

She peeked over her shoulder. "Everything okay back there?"

"Define 'okay.'" His voice echoed from the closet. "There's a whole saxophone section in here. I think they're multiplying."

Elaine laughed, walking over. "Need backup?"

He stepped out with a clarinet case in hand, brushing cobwebs from the top. "I'm fine. Just... realizing I've inherited more than I thought."

"You don't have to do it all at once," she said. "Even a song takes time to warm up."

Tom looked at the case for a long moment, then placed it on the counter. Elaine noticed the way his fingers lingered on the worn leather handle.

She wondered what memories were woven into that handle, the silent stories housed in the worn leather. More about the life that once brought music to the clarinet, rather than the instrument itself.

A little later, after she finished hanging a garland of fabric stars across her booth, Elaine took her tea to the back and followed the faintest sound. It was notes playing soft, low, and almost inaudible. She could not find the sound, yet enjoyed listening to it.

The shop had fallen quiet, save for a mellow, breathy tune drifting in from the main room. She stood still in the doorway, just out of sight.

Tom was sitting on the piano bench with the clarinet in his lap, his head bowed, eyes closed. His fingers moved with quiet precision, coaxing a gentle melody from the reed. It was haunting and sweet, wrapped in memory. It wasn't polished, but it was human. Vulnerable. Real.

Elaine didn't move. She didn't want to interrupt what made him lift that instrument again.

After a few bars, he stopped and let out a breath, unaware of his audience. Elaine stepped forward, not wanting to startle him. "That was beautiful," she said.

Tom was surprised and straightened up. "I didn't know you were listening."

"I wasn't," she replied. "I was feeling."

He looked down at the clarinet. "It was nothing. Just... air and old habits."

"I think it was something." She folded her arms. "You should play at the exhibit."

Her tone was light, supportive, but her eyes held a quiet encouragement. She wasn't teasing. She saw something worth sharing, honest and stirring.

Tom picked up on what she was expressing, then he scoffed. "Yeah, that's not happening."

Elaine tilted her head. "Why not? It's clear to me you still have the music in you."

"That was just me fooling around. Nobody needs to hear that."

She gave a small shrug and walked back to her table. "Suit yourself. But just so you know, that kind of 'fooling around' would make people linger. It tells a story without saying a word. Do you know how many people would enjoy listening to you play?"

Tom stood up, tucking the clarinet back into its case. "I'm not the storytelling type."

"You say that," Elaine replied, arranging a stack of folded quilts, "but you don't seem to mind building a stage for everyone else. Storytellers do that."

He paused. "It's easier that way. But not always more meaningful."

"But not always better," she said.

Their eyes met for a moment, too long to be casual, too short to be anything more. Elaine turned back to her booth, smoothing a wrinkle from a table runner with more attention than was necessary.

Throughout the day, customers came in and out of the music shop. The subtle background of Christmas music brought smiles to everyone who entered. They shared stories of their Christmas traditions, and several purchases were made, including Christmas albums and CDs.

After a while, Tom joined her, setting down a small box of wire hooks and card stands.

"You planning to label each piece?" he asked.

Elaine nodded. "A title, maybe a short backstory. People like knowing there's meaning behind what they touch."

He picked up a small woven square with threads of deep green and copper. "What's this one?"

Elaine smiled. "That's 'Forest After Rain.' It's based on a morning I spent hiking near a glen in Ireland. The mist, the silence, my time there felt... sacred."

Tom studied the piece. "I can see that. It feels... peaceful."

She tucked a strand of hair behind her ear with sudden shyness. "I make things to capture moments. You play them. Both ways of storytelling."

He gave her a sideways glance. "We're not so different then, huh?"

"Nope. Just using different tools."

There was a pause. The silence didn't feel empty; it felt charged, like the pause between notes. Elaine reached for a notepad and scribbled down display tags, while Tom walked a slow circuit around the space, testing for uneven floorboards and checking sightlines. Every now and then, he'd glance her way, as if checking to make sure she was still real, still choosing to spend her mornings in his father's old shop.

"You think people would want to hear me play?" he asked with curiosity.

She looked up. "Yes. I do."

Tom didn't reply, but he didn't dismiss it either.

Later, as the day continued and golden light filtered through the windows, their rhythm settled into something companionable. They moved around each other, passing scissors, shifting chairs, making notes. At one point, they reached for the same display riser, and their hands brushed. Neither pulled away as they each assessed the moment.

Elaine felt the blush creep onto her cheeks first. "Careful. People might think we're enjoying ourselves."

Tom chuckled. "Dangerous territory."

"But not the worst kind."

He met her gaze, and something unspoken passed between them. Amusement, curiosity, maybe even a thread of something warmer, not yet quite formed.

She cleared her throat. "Well, if we're almost done for the day, I might pop next door for a hot chocolate."

Tom glanced at the clock. "You've earned it."

She slid her coat on but lingered near the door. "Same time tomorrow?"

He nodded. "Wouldn't miss it."

Elaine stepped outside into the soft hush of late afternoon snow. As she walked down Harmony Lane, cup of hot chocolate warming her hands, she thought of the music she'd heard today. Not just Tom's clarinet, but the rhythm of two people learning how to share space, how to listen, how to create something meaningful together. The customers that came in and out of the shop were welcomed, and some even shared their stories of music with us.

The lights twinkled along the eaves of the shops, and distant laughter from the café made the street feel alive. A couple walked past hand in hand, their scarves trailing behind them in the wind. Elaine took it all in. The sights, the sounds, the way Harmony Lane breathed with inner warmth.

She wasn't just documenting this season as she previously did. She was living it.

And though she wouldn't say it out loud, not yet, she already knew what she'd title the next piece in her collection.

"Quiet Reeds."

Elaine wandered down the street, her boots leaving impressions in the fresh snow. Instead of heading straight back to the cottage, she took a detour along the trail that wound behind the row of shops. There, the trees stood quiet and still, branches laden with snow like sleeping sentinels. She paused by a snow-covered bench and sat, the cold seeping through her coat, grounding her.

It had been years since she'd felt this kind of peace, unforced, unexpected. Most of her life had been in motion, cataloged through lenses and lighting, the rush of deadlines pressing at her back. But Harmony Lane moved at a different rhythm. Here, stillness wasn't absence. It was presence. Presence of care, of community, of moments that didn't need to be captured to be meaningful.

She pulled a small sketchbook from her coat pocket and drew a few soft lines. The angle of Tom's clarinet as he played, the curl of a garland she'd hung, the light streaming through the front window like honey through gauze. Her fingers moved on instinct, capturing feeling more than detail. These weren't designs for the booth. They were something else entirely.

When she stood up, the cold had numbed her legs, and her heart had softened. She walked home with snowflakes catching on her lashes.

Back at the cottage, she left the lights low. The hearth glowed with embers from her earlier fire, and she curled up under a quilt with a mug of warmed cider. She replayed the day in her mind, not the tasks, but the **moments** like the way Tom's voice grew steadier with every suggestion. The look on his face when she complimented his playing. And when their hands had brushed, neither had apologized.

She let out a laugh and shook her head as she recalled, "Dangerous territory," he'd said.

Maybe. But not unfamiliar.

She continued her thought of Tom for a moment, recalling his reserved strength and gentle teasing. She thought about how he looked at her across the table when she was lost in thought. For years, she had convinced herself that kind of connection was behind her. A chapter closed. But Tom wasn't trying to replace anyone, and she wasn't trying to resurrect the past. What was beginning between them felt slow, unspoken, and full of its own kind of grace.

That night, she dreamed of snow-covered fields stitched with golden thread. Of music floating upward like breath in winter. Of hands creating and hearts unfolding.

The next morning, the wind had calmed, and the sky opened into a gentle blue. Elaine stepped outside with a purpose. Her sketchbook was tucked beneath her arm, a bundle of new fabrics in hand. When she reached Melody's, she saw Tom inside, turning on the lights.

He turned around as she entered, surprise flashing across his face before it settled into something warmer. "You're early."

"So are you."

He gestured to the kettle. "Holiday Blend tea this time."

She smiled. "Progress."

As they set about arranging more displays and refining the layout, the rhythm resumed, comfortable and purposeful. Between tasks and customers, they shared snippets of memories. Tom told her about the time he'd played clarinet in a hotel lobby during a snowstorm, stranded with concerned travelers. Elaine shared a story about an artist she'd met in Morocco who dyed silk using spices and wildflowers.

Every story deepened the threads between them, stitching their lives in ways neither had expected.

That afternoon, she pinned a note on the corner of her booth. It read:

"Places That Hold Us – Handwoven pieces from journeys of the heart."

Tom read it and nodded. "I like that. You'll draw a crowd."

"You should add your own note."

He shook his head but didn't argue.

Elaine tilted hers. "What would it say if you did?"

Tom hesitated, then shrugged. "Songs I never planned to share."

She smiled. "Those are the best kind."

And for the first time, Tom didn't deflect. He nodded and returned to stringing lights, their glow catching in the corners of the room like small promises waiting to be kept.

Snowfall and Doubts

ELAINE WOKE UP TO the gentle hush of snow falling outside her window. The quiet that blanketed the town made even the birds pause their morning chatter. Today's fresh snow coated rooftops and sidewalks into frosted confections as it fell on Harmony Lane. She pulled the curtains aside to find the lane washed in white, the trees bowing under gentle weight, the shop signs haloed with fluffy drifts. Everything looked softer, touched by a kind of magic only winter could deliver.

She wrapped herself in a shawl and stood by the window for a moment, tea warming her hands. Her breath fogged the glass as she watched a child twirl in the falling snow, arms outstretched, pure delight etched across her face. A smile tugged at Elaine's lips. Snow had a way of softening the edges of landscapes and hearts alike.

She sipped her tea, savoring the quiet. In her travel years, snow days meant canceled flights and disrupted plans, but here, they offered an invitation—an excuse to stay home, slow down, and notice. She thought of how the snow softened the outlines of every roof and lamppost, just as her time on Harmony Lane was softening the edges of her past. It reminded her it was okay to let go of the rush and to let the silence speak. There were no deadlines here, only the whisper of wind through pines and the hush of her own heart learning how to listen again.

Over at Melody's Vintage Music & Arts, Tom arrived early, brushing snow from the stoop with deliberate swipes. The shop felt different today. The snow muted the town, wrapping around the building. Inside, the store offered a warm welcome from the cold. The stillness awaited the activity of a new day. As he looked out the big front window, the other store's twinkling lights looked brighter than usual. *Perhaps it was enhanced by the snow as the darkness receded*, he thought.

Tom turned on the lights and filled the kettle; the routine had become second nature. As steam rose, he leaned against the counter and caught sight of an old framed photo tucked behind a stack of ledgers. He was careful as he pulled it out.

A twenty-year-younger version of himself stared back at him, standing with a jazz trio, clarinet in hand, a rare smile on his face. The photo was taken in Chicago during one of the better winters, back when he still believed in sharing music with everyone. He felt a pang, the kind of ache that surfaced when you saw something you'd left behind. A part of yourself you hadn't realized was still there. Before life offered enough disappointment to make him tuck it away.

He remembered that night as if it were yesterday. The velvet stage curtains, the way the reed squeaked during the second number, and how the older man in the front row hummed along to every song. They'd played to a small but warm crowd, and when it was over, someone asked for an encore. That was the last time Tom performed without reservation. Somewhere after that came the heartbreak, the burned-out years, the silence. He hadn't stopped playing, just stopped sharing. Then he realized a familiar song playing in the background, one he played many years ago.

He didn't hear Elaine enter the shop, lost in the memories of that song playing until she shut the door behind her. Snow clung to her scarf and settled like stardust in her curls.

"Good morning," she said, stamping her boots on the mat.

He held up the photo. "Look what I found."

Elaine stepped closer, studying the image. "Is that you? I love the suit."

"It was rented," Tom said, smiling. "But yeah. That was twenty years back, a lifetime ago."

"You look happy."

He nodded, returning the frame to the counter. "I was. Back then, music didn't feel like such a risk."

Elaine poured water into two mugs, catching the smell as it flowed over the bags, her touch familiar with the rhythm of the store. "What changed?"

Tom stirred his mug. "Somewhere along the line, I stopped thinking anyone needed to hear what I wanted to play. And then it became easier not to play anything at all."

Elaine picked up her mug. "I don't think it's ever about whether people need to hear it. It's about whether *you* need to play it. The music falls on the ears who need it."

They sat by the window, the falling snow casting a soft glow through the glass. Silence sat between them, broken only by the occasional sips of tea or creaks of the old radiator.

"The Christmas lights in the store windows look brighter today,"

Elaine said.

"I suppose so, it looked that way to me earlier," Tom replied.

Elaine reached into her tote and pulled out a piece of soft linen stretched over a frame. Delicate stitches trailed across the fabric like notes in a melody, each thread a whisper of color: slate blue, pine green, warm taupe.

"It's inspired by this town," she said. "By this street, the people, the feeling of... belonging."

Tom studied the growing tapestry. "What are you calling it?"

"Haven't decided yet. Maybe 'Winter's Welcome.' Or 'First Snow.'" She paused. "Or maybe 'Harmony.'"

Tom's eyes lingered on her work. "It fits. You capture things that most people would miss."

Elaine glanced at him. "Like music heard through closed doors?"

A smile pulled at one corner of his mouth. "Touché."

The day passed in gentle waves. Customers came and went, often in pairs, encouraged by the slow cadence of the snow. Each time the bell above the door rang, it added to the activity of the day. Elaine worked at her stitching between conversations, while Tom rearranged the displays and checked the lighting for best positioning.

A young boy came in with his grandmother, both bundled tight in wool scarves. The boy asked if the saxophone on the shelf could play jazz like in the movies. Tom kneeled down and explained the basics, his voice gentler than Elaine had heard before. The grandmother bought a sheet of vintage holiday music "just for nostalgia," she said with a wink. Later, a pair of teenage girls browsed the handmade ornaments, giggling as they squabbled over which one would look best on their

Christmas tree. Elaine smiled to herself, stitching as they continued. The shop had become more than a workspace; it was becoming a gathering place.

In the mid-afternoon, the snowfall thickened. Through the front window, Harmony Lane blurred into a watercolor of whites and grays. Elaine looked up. "Think we'll get snowed in?"

Tom checked his phone. "Forecast says it's temporary. But you're welcome to stay until it lets up."

Elaine smiled. "I might take you up on that. The cottage is lovely, but it's drafty. Your tea stash has gotten better here, too."

They shared a laugh, then settled again into their tasks.

Tom glanced at the old photo he had found earlier once more. "Do you ever miss it? The rush of it all? Your old life?"

Elaine considered. "I miss the moments that made it memorable. The light just before sunset in the Andes. The silence of the Sahara at dawn. But I don't miss the pace. Or the loneliness that came with always being the observer."

Tom nodded. "I used to think staying still meant giving up. Turns out, it just gives things time to settle."

He walked over to the shelf, pulled out a weathered clarinet case, and placed it on the counter. Elaine's eyes widened, but she didn't say a word.

"I'm not making any promises," Tom said.

She raised her hands in mock surrender. "I'm just here for the tea and the stitching. And our discussions."

He smiled as he opened the case and took out the instrument. After a few adjustments and a soft breath, he played a few notes. Not a full song, just a wandering melody that rose and fell like falling snow. It wasn't polished, but it was honest.

The melody wavered, unhurried, aching, intimate. Elaine felt it settle low in her chest, awakening something tender. Her fingers, usually so steady, hovered above the fabric, unwilling to break the moment. The shop seemed to inhale the sound, holding it close. Even the snow outside looked like it slowed to listen. She didn't dare speak right away when he finished. Music like that wasn't meant to be answered with words.

Elaine paused her stitching and listened, her heart catching in the space between notes.

When he finished, the room felt different. Lighter somehow.

"You're still in there," she said.

He gave a small nod. "I just needed a quiet place to hear myself again."

Elaine returned to her stitching, her fingers steady, her heart full. She decided to call this piece *Harmony*, and she knew why.

Outside, the snow slowed, the sky lightened enough to hint at the return of the sun. Inside, the shop was a sanctuary. Not just for instruments and fabric, but for two souls rediscovering the beauty of being seen.

Elaine glanced over her shoulder at Tom, still holding the clarinet as if unsure whether to put it away. "You know," she said, "you might want to think about a set list."

He was still dealing with his own uncertainty and groaned. "Don't push your luck."

She grinned. "That's what makes it fun."

The day ended with more light than when it began. They said their goodbyes. As Elaine stepped out into the snowy evening, the warmth of the shop lingered in her bones. Her breath curled into the sky, and her footsteps left impressions like breadcrumbs on the path home.

Back at the cottage, she hung her half-finished piece on the wall above the fireplace—threads of color against linen. Memory and hope sewn side by side. She stepped back, studied it, then picked up a pencil and wrote its title in her sketchbook.

She thought back to the moment Tom played, how vulnerable it felt, how beautifully uncertain. It reminded her of her first gallery show years ago, her palms damp as she watched strangers examine her work. That same mixture of pride and terror. Creating was always an act of bravery. Sharing it even more so. It was as if Harmony Lane was inviting her to be brave again. Not as a traveler or an observer, but as someone who belonged here. Perhaps she might stay.

"Harmony." That's what she wrote in her sketchbook.

More snow fell, and with it, the real stirrings of something new.

Hidden Notes

THE SNOW HAD STOPPED overnight, leaving behind a hushed town wrapped in white. The sun broke through by midmorning, turning Harmony Lane into a corridor of light and shimmer. Elaine stepped outside with a hopeful feeling in her chest. There was something about the way the air smelled here. Clean, pine-laced, full of possibility. That made her feel bold.

She stood for a moment at the edge of her porch, feeling the crisp air bite her cheeks. Memories of snowy mornings in faraway places flickered to mind: the early market calls in Norway, a frost-covered tent flap in Mongolia, the quiet hush of snowfall in Prague. Yet, none of these quite matched this moment. Those days were full of movement, chasing stories and fleeting times. Harmony Lane, by contrast, was stillness with potential. She hadn't realized until now how much she'd longed for something slower, grounded.

She stopped by the music shop with a simple idea tucked into her back pocket. The holiday concert was this weekend, a neighborhood tradition held in the community room above the cafe. A handful of locals played familiar carols and folk tunes while others brought cookies, cider, or good cheer. It was casual, cozy, and joyfully imperfect, what memories are made of.

Elaine helped string a few final paper lanterns along the windowsills, their glow casting soft halos on the faces already gathered. Someone tuned a banjo in the corner, and children darted between adults with napkins in hand, collecting gingerbread cookies like treasures. Near the back, a couple clinked mugs of cider and swayed in time to the music, even before it began. This wasn't just a concert; it was the heartbeat of the town, stitched together by memory and melody. The smell of warm cider mixed with the sweetness of gingerbread, while the low hum of voices added a layer of comfort to the room.

Volunteers moved chairs closer together to make room for last-minute arrivals, and Elaine noticed how easily people settled into shared space. A woman handed out programs with hand-stamped snowflakes and other decorations. A teenager with rosy cheeks offered peppermint bark from a basket lined with red flannel. Every detail, from the cracked piano bench to the mismatched mugs, told the same story: this was a place where everyone belonged, imperfections and all.

Elaine pushed open the door to Melody's, the bell chiming as usual. Tom looked up from the register where he was sorting through a stack of donation receipts.

The shop glowed with a kind of winter warmth that only old wood and soft lighting could provide. Dust motes hovered in sunbeams like snowflakes paused midair. The brass of the old instruments shimmered, while the scent of cinnamon from the brewed tea lingered in the corners. Elaine felt a familiar peace settle over her. This place had become a kind of anchor, even in its quiet chaos.

"Good morning," she said. "I have a proposition."

Tom raised an eyebrow. "That sounds dangerous."

"Harmless, I promise. There's a concert this Saturday, just a casual neighborhood thing above the cafe. A few folks are bringing instruments, nothing formal. I thought you might want to come."

His body stilled. He set the receipts down. "To watch?"

"To listen. To maybe play, if the mood strikes."

Tom leaned back against the counter, arms crossed. "Elaine..."

She held up a hand. "No pressure. Just an invitation. Sometimes music sounds different in a room full of friends."

He looked out the window for a long beat before answering. Tom was conflicted. He couldn't wait to play and yet felt quite restricted, but was unsure why. *A memory crossed his mind as he thought about it.* "I don't know. I'm not sure I'd even remember how to keep up with a group."

"That's the beauty of it," she said. "No one cares. There's no set list, no rehearsal. Just music for the sake of joy."

He smiled. "You make it sound easy."

"Not easy, just... welcome."

He didn't say yes, but he didn't say no either. Still battling with his feelings.

After Elaine left the shop, Tom stood alone behind the counter, gazing at the door long after it closed. He set the receipts aside and walked to the back room, where his clarinet case sat on a shelf, untouched since arriving in Harmony Lane after his dad passed. He ran a hand over it, not opening it, not yet. There was a time when performing felt like second nature, like breathing. A bridge to a past he wasn't sure he could reclaim. Now, it felt more like remembering how to start again. But her invitation unsettled something in him enough to make him question whether silencing his music had been the right choice. A faint pull toward the part of himself he'd left dormant. That night, he sat by the fireplace with the case nearby. He sipped his tea, debating whether a quiet life meant silencing his song or if it was time to begin again.

By Saturday evening, the second floor of the cafe buzzed with energy. Paper snowflakes dangled from the rafters, and twinkling lights framed the makeshift stage: a rug, two mic stands, and an upright piano that wheezed on low notes. Children bundled in fleece sprawled on the floor with mugs of cocoa, and the smell of gingerbread hovered like perfume.

Elaine chatted with Carol, who had arrived with a tray of cranberry scones and an encouraging grin. "Think he'll show?" Carol asked.

Elaine glanced at the stairs. "I don't know. But I left the invitation open."

Carol followed her gaze, then nudged her. "You've got a look about you."

"What look?" Elaine asked, sipping from her cup.

"The hopeful kind. Like someone waiting for a second verse of a song they thought had ended."

Elaine laughed. "You've been spending too much time around lyrics."

"Maybe. But I know my sister. And I know you don't issue casual invitations."

A guitar duo played a cheerful rendition of "Let It Snow," followed by an older woman who played a spirited harmonica solo that got a standing ovation. People clapped along, voices rose in soft harmonies, and the room swayed with good humor.

Elaine began to relax when she heard a sound on the staircase behind her. She turned. There was Tom, wearing a simple charcoal sweater and holding a weathered clarinet case.

He looked uncomfortable but resolute, like someone who had faced something old and heavy.

Elaine walked over to him. "You came."

He gave her a quiet nod. "I almost didn't."

She smiled. "But you did."

He stood near the back at first, leaning against a post as the next song began. Then, as if pulled by some invisible string, he went to the side of the stage and opened the case.

No one made a fuss. No spotlight turned. The crowd continued their chatter in between sips, but something shifted when the first notes floated out of Tom's clarinet, soft, low, lingering, and clear.

It was a simple melody, perhaps a lullaby of sorts. Gentle, searching. The tune that quiets a room not by volume, but by depth.

Elaine felt as if she had stopped breathing. Not because of the music itself, but because of what it cost him to play it. The music was vulnerable, coming alive from the sheets of music. Honest. Alive!

The last note hung in the air like a question. Then someone clapped. Then another. And soon, the room filled with warm applause, not thunderous, but steady, grateful.

Tom gave a short nod, his face unreadable, and stepped down.

Elaine met him halfway. "That was beautiful."

Tom looked at the floor, the clarinet still in his hand. "I wasn't sure I could still do it. My hands were shaking before I even began."

Elaine touched his elbow. "That made it even more powerful. Everyone felt it."

He shook his head with a quiet laugh. "I thought I'd feel relief when it was over. But instead, I just..." He paused, eyes far away. "I felt seen."

He shrugged. "It felt... strange."

"In a good way?"

He hesitated. "In an authentic way."

They moved to the back of the room and, for a while, enjoyed listening to others play. As the night unfolded, the room seemed to take on a new kind of energy. Each song, no matter how imperfect, added another layer to the community's heartbeat.

A boy no older than nine played a short piano piece, his legs swinging beneath the bench. He missed a few notes, but the crowd clapped as if he'd conquered Carnegie Hall. His father snapped a picture and wiped his eyes. Next, a woman in her seventies sang an a cappella version of "O Holy Night." Her voice weathered but steady. The room hushed around her, reverent.

Elaine leaned in close and whispered, "This town may not have spotlights, but it sure knows how to shine." Tom nodded. "Everyone brings their own kind of light." A teenage girl performed an original song on an acoustic guitar. A trio of siblings sang a carol out of tune. It didn't matter. Every moment added something human to the evening.

Afterward, they walked side by side down the snowy sidewalk, the town hushed again beneath a silver sky. Shop windows flickered with warmth, and the music from earlier seemed to follow them like an echo.

A breeze lifted the loose snowflakes from nearby awnings, sending them dancing between streetlamps. The shop windows spilled golden light across the sidewalk. They passed a bakery where someone inside waved; Tom nodded back, unfamiliar but acknowledged. "I used to walk through places like this on tour," he said. "But I never stayed long enough to recognize anyone's face. Tonight felt... different."

Elaine smiled. "Maybe this is the kind of tour that doesn't require you to leave."

Tom broke the silence. "I used to think I missed the music. But I think I missed being heard."

Elaine touched his arm. "I'm sure. And it could also be the music missed you, too."

They paused at the corner where the lane split toward the cottages and the shop. He turned to her, eyes earnest.

"Maybe... I could play one piece at the Christmas exhibit. Just one. Nothing big."

Her smile spread like warmth through wool. "I think that would be more than enough."

They said goodnight, not with a hug or promise, but with a shared understanding.

Tom lingered a moment after she turned down the path toward her cottage. He looked up at the sky, where stars peeked out through drifting clouds, and exhaled. His breath rose and disappeared into the night, but the warmth in his chest remained. Maybe the past didn't have to be something he left behind. Maybe it could be something he carried forward: one note, one moment, one shared glance at a time. There was a shift. A door cracked open. A sound returned.

Elaine walked home with the quiet satisfaction of a note well played.

As she crossed the lane, her footsteps slow and deliberate, she caught a glimpse of her reflection in a darkened shop window. She looked... different. Not younger, not changed beyond recognition. Just present. Grounded. It had been years since she'd felt that way. Not caught between flights, or juggling edits, or sleeping in unfamiliar beds. This was different. Harmony Lane was stitching itself into her, one snow-covered step at a time. Harmony Lane gleamed under the moonlight, and for the first time in years, so did possibility.

Back at her cottage, she wrote in her notebook: "We carry our stories in sound and stitch. And sometimes, we find the courage to let them be heard."

She set the notebook down and crossed to the window, watching the gentle swirl of snow. Lights from the street cast a golden hue onto the flakes, turning the night into something luminous. She thought of the first day she'd arrived on Harmony Lane. How the cottage had felt foreign and still. Now it felt like home, being filled with moments that mattered.

She walked back to the fireplace, where her latest weaving was resting over the back of a chair. Her fingers moved, trailing across the threads. This one wasn't from a faraway land or an ancient market. It was from here. From this new rhythm, she was learning to trust.

She whispered into the quiet, more to herself than the room, "Let it keep going."

Outside, snow began again, light, unhurried.

The rhythm of a town, and two hearts, continuing.

Twinkling Lights and Tapestries

ELAINE STOOD IN THE center of Melody's Music & Arts, arms crossed over her chest, surveying the space that had become almost as familiar to her as her own cottage. Outside, the snow was falling again. Thick flakes drifted past the windows like feathers. The town went quiet, the way it often did during December on Harmony Lane, where time moved like molasses and every little detail seemed to matter more. She could hear the soft crunch of footsteps from the sidewalk and the occasional shout of Christmas cheer as people passed the stores along the street. With its timeless charm, the town seemed to expect something lovely everywhere they went. The holiday exhibit was just days away, and the stores buzzed with preparations. Everyone's attention was drawn to the lights and colors as they walked around town. There were memories to be made wherever they went. Some stores had traditional Christmas music, while others added newer tunes to the mix. Elaine directed her attention back to the tables pushed against the walls. Every corner of the store embraced Christmas. New lighting was being tested, and display pieces were arranged in careful stacks around the perimeter of the room like performers waiting for their cue.

She took a deep breath, smelling wood polish, cinnamon, and fabric dye blending together as a new holiday aroma. Her corner had taken shape: woven hangings in indigo, copper, and cream swayed from wooden rods, catching light in subtle ways, inviting touch as much as admiration. Each textile was paired with a handwritten card, describing not just the materials and dyes but also the story behind it. The markets in Morocco, the ocean winds of the Pacific coast, the burst of color in Jaipur.

She paused to run her hands along a bolt of raw linen waiting to be stretched on a frame. She hadn't planned on bringing this one. It was an unfinished piece she began during her travels. Woven with uneven tension and threads of uncertainty, was a reminder of a time when she didn't quite know where she was heading. But something about Harmony Lane had urged her to bring it today. Maybe because this town, with its quiet charm and slower rhythm, was helping her find closure in the things she thought she'd abandoned. Maybe she'll even finish it tonight.

Elaine stepped back to adjust one of the fabric labels. Her hands lingered on the edge of a vibrant scarf dyed in shades of rose and plum. It was one of her favorites. Stitched during her last trip abroad before deciding to settle, though she hadn't realized it at the time. A woman paused nearby to study it.

"This one feels... familiar," the woman whispered. "Warm, like something cherished."

Elaine smiled. "That was India. I stitched it during the monsoon season. I remember the rain sounding like constant applause on the rooftops."

The woman pressed a hand to her heart. "You can feel that in the threads."

Elaine watched her move on, a quiet joy blooming in her chest. It wasn't just art. It was understood. Each of these pieces speak on a different level, and with a different feeling. She lingered beside the display, straightening one of the story cards that had curled at the corner. Her eyes traced the fabric she had dyed by hand under a sky filled with thunder. For a moment, she was back there in that open-air market with voices all around, the smell of mangoes and spice, the hum of scooters buzzing past. And now, here it was, on display so far away, in a shop on Harmony Lane. She had traveled far and wide, but this moment, this connection with a stranger over a scarf, felt like a kind of homecoming.

Just then, Carol stepped through the front door, bringing with her a swirl of snowflakes and her signature cheer. "It looks and feels magical in here," she said, pulling off her gloves. "Like a snow globe someone wished into existence."

Elaine chuckled. "We're almost there. Just a few finishing touches."

Carol wandered toward the tapestries, her fingers brushing over a deep blue weaving with silver accents. "Your work brings out a kind of stillness in people. Like it makes them pause. That's a gift, you know."

Elaine felt a wave of warmth. "I used to chase wonder across the world. Maybe it was always about bringing it back home. Maybe I was meant to find it right here."

They shared a quiet and understanding look. Then Carol moved on to chat with the young artist arranging his prints by the register, and Elaine returned to her corner of the store.

As she kneeled to tape down an edge of cloth that had curled, her eyes lingered on the floorboards. They were scuffed in places, marked with years of footsteps and rearrangements, but there was history in those imperfections. She thought of the other artists who had passed through here. Musicians, painters, poets, all leaving some of themselves behind. She smiled at the idea of adding her thread to that tapestry.

In the back room, Tom stood alone with his clarinet. He'd spent the past few mornings arriving early, playing while the town was still asleep. He never played more than a few bars at a time—scales, fragments of lullabies, the faint echo of something he'd once composed and never finished. The notes didn't come easy at first. His breath felt unsure, his fingers not quite obedient, attempting to reclaim something he'd almost forgotten how to reach for. But the act of doing, of coaxing sound from silence, had become its own kind of ritual.

Sometimes after playing, he would stand by the rear window and look out over the alleyway lined with frosted garbage bins and tired ivy. It wasn't scenic, but it gave him perspective, reminding him that beauty didn't always arrive in sweeping views or perfect timing. It came in showing up.

This morning, he almost played a full song before losing his nerve. The melody faltered near the bridge, and he paused, feeling foolish despite the empty room.

He lowered the clarinet, frustration creasing his brow. "You're not on a stage," he muttered to himself. "It's just wood and reed. It's just you." He sat on the stool beside him and rested the clarinet across his lap. Memories flickered to his first solo at nineteen, his father clapping from the second row, the feel of velvet curtains behind his back. Then, in later years, the stage became harder to approach. Not because of the audience, but because of what he believed the audience expected.

He closed his eyes for a moment, letting the silence wrap around him like a jacket. Maybe it wasn't about performance anymore. Maybe it was about presence, and allowing the music to find him again.

He stood and walked to a small shelf where a dusty notebook sat, its pages filled with old compositions and forgotten thoughts. Flipping through it, he paused on a half-finished piece written in longhand, the ink faded but legible. With a pencil, he sketched in a few missing notes. It didn't need to be perfect. It just needed to be honest.

Before returning to the front room, Tom lingered another minute, cradling the clarinet in both hands. He blew across the mouthpiece and played a single, sustained note. It wavered at first, then steadied into something smooth and warm. He held it longer than usual, letting it carry the weight of his hesitation, like the hanging note in a Mozart piece. When it faded, the room didn't feel so empty. The warmth of the note's energy was absorbed into the room.

He set the clarinet down and returned to the main room, where Elaine stood repositioning a narrow weaving across a paneled backdrop.

"Need help?" he asked, startling her.

She turned with a smile. "Only if you're volunteering."

"Sort of a package deal at this point, isn't it?"

She handed him the top edge of the textile. "Lift this just an inch... a little more... perfect."

They adjusted the display in silence within a few moments. The nearness felt familiar now, but still held a gentle current neither had dared to name.

Elaine stepped back and gave him a thoughtful look. "Have you practiced today?"

He gave a slight shrug. "Maybe."

Her voice was soft. "You don't have to prove anything, you know. Showing up counts."

Tom nodded but didn't respond right away. He walked over to a crate, grabbing the string of lights. "Where do these go?"

She gestured to the front window. "I thought we'd wrap the window frame and hang a few low, like starlight."

He went to the window, unwinding the lights. "Are you enjoying being here for Christmas?"

Elaine paused. "At first I wasn't, but my sister, Carol, gave me the flyer about the Annual Indoor Christmas Art & Music Exhibit, and that's what led me to your store."

She added, "With each passing day, my heart grows fonder of this place and spending time with you here."

He glanced over his shoulder. "I am glad you are here, too."

"I'm still learning what this is. But it feels like something good."

They worked in tandem, wrapping the lights, stepping around one another. Tom pulled a small step stool from the corner and climbed up to secure the final loop around the window frame. Elaine held the string steady, glancing up every so often to catch the shape of his profile against the twilight. His brow was furrowed in concentration, his breath visible in the cool air near the glass.

As they decorated, they shared their life stories with each other. Elaine spoke of her time in the Pacific Northwest, where weaving first claimed her attention in a way that no other craft had. Tom recalled the first time he heard a symphony as a boy, not understanding all the instruments but feeling them vibrate in his chest like a language he'd always known.

At one point, Tom's hand brushed hers. Neither moved. The contact was brief, accidental, but neither spoke. The silence filled with something heavier than words. For a moment, the world beyond the shop window seemed to slow, and the only sound was the faint clink of bulbs swaying against the glass.

Elaine cleared her throat. "I made something for you."

Tom blinked. "You did?"

She walked to the counter and pulled a small bundle wrapped in kraft paper and tied with jute string. "Don't open it yet. Wait until you're alone. But it's... it's from what I've been feeling since I heard you play."

He accepted the gift as if it might dissolve. "Thank you."

"You're welcome."

For a moment, they just stood there, the lights casting a soft glow across their faces. The shop was quiet, bathed in the amber hue of late afternoon. A song played from the old stereo in the corner, instrumental, soft jazz, unhurried.

Elaine turned back to her display. "We're almost ready, aren't we?"

Tom nodded. "More than I expected to be, because of your help."

As the daylight dimmed and the last of the displays found their places, the shop took on the feeling of something sacred. Not grand or polished, but genuine. Like a heartbeat made visible.

Elaine stepped outside to see how the window looked from the street. Inside, Tom was adjusting the last strand of lights, reflecting his face shimmering in the glass, half-lit by the golden glow.

She pressed her gloved hand to the window.

Inside, Tom looked up and smiled.

The lights twinkled. The tapestries swayed. And the space between them continued to shrink, one quiet moment at a time. Outside, the snow deepened, covering the sidewalks despite a mild breeze. The glow from Melody's spilled onto the lane like a golden ribbon, illuminating the tracks of late walkers and curious children with mittened hands pressed to the glass. Inside, in the calm after creation, the air pulsed with an energy unsaid but felt. A melody waiting for its second verse. A scarf not yet unwrapped. And the quiet possibility that two people who had spent years hiding different parts of themselves were beginning to be seen, fully, and without fear.

And beneath it all, in the gentle hush of Harmony Lane, something invisible but unmistakable took root, not fireworks, not declarations. Just the quiet understanding that some beginnings don't come with fanfare. They come with light. And time. And shared glances across a room full of hope.

Hearts on Display

THE GLOW OF MELODY's Music & Arts spilled onto Harmony Lane like golden thread woven through a tapestry of snow and song. Evening had fallen with quiet grace, and the holiday exhibit had arrived. Warm light flickered from each windowpane, spilling across the sidewalk where guests shuffled inside in wool coats and scarves, their laughter trailing behind them like ribbon.

Elaine stood just inside the entrance, welcoming visitors with a quiet smile. The store was transformed, alive with color, light, and music. Every wall shimmered with artwork. Candles flickered on tabletops beside mugs of cider and sprigs of pine. A low hum of holiday jazz wrapped around the room, comforting as a well-worn quilt. She took a deep breath, letting it settle in. This moment, this gathering, this feeling of shared warmth and wonder. It was everything she hadn't realized she missed.

Guests wandered from table to table, admiring pottery, illustrations, ornaments, and more. But it was Elaine's booth that seemed to gather a steady crowd. Her tapestries hung like old souls on the walls, threaded with indigo skies, earthen tones, and untold stories. Each piece had a small card detailing its inspiration. Travelers read, some aloud, some with furrowed brows that softened into smiles.

A teenage girl stood transfixed before a crimson-and-gold weave. "It looks like fire and rain at the same time," she said.

Elaine stepped beside her. "That one's from Morocco. A storm rolled through the desert while I worked on it. All color and chaos, but beautiful in its own way."

The girl grinned. "It's like it's still alive."

Elaine smiled. That was the highest compliment her work could receive: someone else seeing the soul she had woven into it.

Nearby, two older women lingered by a tapestry woven in shades of ocean green and misty gray.

"Reminds me of Oregon," one said. "Cannon Beach, maybe?"

Elaine overheard and walked over. "It is," she said. "I spent three weeks there during the rainy season. That color came from foraged blackberries and rusted iron."

The women looked at her in surprise, then wonder. "You made this?"

"I did."

One of them reached out, touching the edge of the weaving. "It feels like the sea is right here in the room."

A soft, melodic tune played in the background, a cello, and piano duet that drifted like snowflakes. Carol moved through the store with a tray of cider refills, pausing now and then to chat with guests. Every inch of the space radiated welcome. It was the kind of evening people would remember as magical.

A group of college students stopped by Elaine's booth next, each drawn to a different piece. One asked about the natural dyes she used, another about the symbolism in a spiral motif. Elaine shared stories she hadn't told in years. Like the time she fell asleep weaving on a rooftop in Thailand, or when a sandstorm in Egypt tried to carry her loom away. The students were captivated, and she was, too, by their curiosity and genuine interest.

In a quieter corner, a local reporter scribbled notes and took photos, nodding as she listened to Carol explain how the exhibit had grown over the years. "There's something different this time," the reporter murmured. "It feels... more personal."

One guest brought her aging mother, who crept through the exhibit with a cane and a quiet sense of awe. When they reached Elaine's booth, the older woman reached out and ran her fingers over a deep plum-and-amber piece.

"This reminds me of my mother's parlor," she whispered. "She had a shawl of this color. I haven't thought about it in years."

Elaine smiled and asked, "Would you like to hear the story behind that one?" The woman nodded, and Elaine spoke, inviting her into the memory.

Nearby, a father knelt beside his young daughter, pointing out distinct patterns and colors as she picked her favorite tapestry. "It's like a treasure map!" the girl exclaimed, her pigtails bouncing with every discovery.

Elaine's heart swelled. These weren't just visitors; they were participants in the magic.

Just then, Carol passed by and whispered, "You've created a corner of the world that feels sacred." Elaine looked at her sister, surprised, and a little moved. "It's not just art. It's a kind of storytelling that invites people to remember who they are."

Her eyes found Tom across the room. He was behind a display table stacked with old sheet music and vintage vinyl. He'd brought them from storage, offering them up as a nostalgic counterpoint to the evening's more contemporary art. But music wasn't on his mind.

His clarinet rested in its case under the table. He hadn't taken it out yet. The idea of performing, of standing up in front of the crowd, even this warm and familiar one, still coiled in his chest.

He busied himself arranging the vinyl records, stealing glances toward Elaine. She was in her element, her fingers dancing over her textiles as she spoke with guests. She looked radiant, like someone who had found her rhythm. And he felt grateful. Anxious. Unmoored.

The old fear tried to creep in. What if he cracked a note? What if the room went quiet in the wrong way? But then he reached for the gift in his coat pocket, the handwoven scarf she'd given him. Tucked away, he remembered her words: *You don't have to prove anything. Just showing up counts.*

At the far end of the store, Carol raised a glass of sparkling cider and tapped a spoon to its rim. The gentle chime hushed the room.

"Friends," she said with a warm smile, "thank you for joining us for our annual Christmas Exhibit. Tonight isn't just about art or music or the beautiful things we create, it's about the way we share them, and the way those things bring us together."

There were murmurs of agreement; it was about the connection it sparked, the stories it called forth. Then a round of applause, awaiting what is next.

"And now," she continued, "we're honored to have a special perfor-mance from someone many of you know. Tom has agreed to share a piece of music tonight, something heartfelt, from his own collection."

Elaine turned toward the back of the room. Tom's eyes met hers, wide and startled. She hadn't known Carol would introduce him like that. But the warmth in the room was palpable. Encouraging.

He took a breath. Then another. Hearing a few people laughing in the silence caused him to tighten up. *Were they laughing at me?* He thought.

He reached down, unlatched the case, and took out the clarinet as he forced those feelings to leave his mind.

The room fell silent. He stepped forward, the floorboards beneath him creaking just enough to remind him he was here, in this moment. No velvet curtain. No spotlight. Just a handmade stage of friends, artists, and a woman in the front row watching him as if he already belonged.

Tom brought the instrument to his lips.

The first note was soft. Delicate. A breath more than a sound. Then came another, fuller, warmer. The melody unfurled like ribbons, smooth and confident, pulling the room, the music, and the people together. He closed his eyes, letting the music lead from his heart.

It wasn't showy. It wasn't perfect. But it was true. The notes told a story of youth and silence, of fear and finding, of life and second chances. This kind of story doesn't need words because everyone al-ready knows it in some corner of their own heart.

Elaine felt tears spring to her eyes. She didn't blink them away. The music plucked at her heartstrings. Others near her were tearing up as well, she observed.

When he finished, there was a beat of silence as if those present let the last note resonate within before their applause. Not the polite kind, but a deeper, warmer, sincere, and sustained applause of appreciation.

Tom bowed his head for a couple of moments, then looked up, and his eyes found hers again. She pressed a hand to her heart. He smiled and thanked everyone for their applause and enjoyment.

The evening carried on, but the room felt different now, more open, more tender. Elaine realized the impact of Tom's music and that it was best for him to start the evening events.

A couple approached Tom with kind words about his music and how long it had been since they had last heard live clarinet. A young boy asked what the instrument was called. Tom kneeled at his level and explained, even letting him touch the keys. It felt good, normal, even.

At Elaine's booth, a man visiting from a gallery in Chicago asked if she would consider commission work. She took his card, her hands a little shaky, and thanked him.

She returned to her booth and found a small note tucked behind one of her weavings. A girl named Hazel had left it, written in loopy cursive: *"Your art made me feel like the world was bigger and smaller at the same time. Thank you."*

Elaine folded the note and slipped it into her pocket. That one would stay with her.

Later, as the guests lingered over the last of the cider and twinkling lights shimmered in the windows, Elaine approached Tom.

"You did it," she said.

He nodded. "It felt... real and made me happy in ways unfelt for years!"

"It was real, and it came from your heart."

They stood together near the front window, the snow continuing to fall, the sound of laughter echoing behind them.

She turned to him again, her voice tentative. "Did you talk to the boy about your clarinet?"

Tom chuckled. "I did."

"He looked at you as if you'd just shown him something magical."

Tom grew quiet, then said, "Maybe that's how I used to look at musicians. Before it all became so... complicated."

Elaine rested a hand on his arm. "Then maybe tonight helped you remember the beginning. The part that wasn't tangled up in expectation."

He nodded, swallowing emotion. "I believe I have."

"And for what it's worth," she added, "your music untangled something in me too."

He looked at her, surprised. She didn't elaborate and was still sorting it out for herself.

A bell above the door jingled as the last guests left, arms full of wrapped art and cider-scented smiles. Carol waved goodnight, mouthing "well done" to both of them before locking the door behind her.

The shop grew quiet. Only the soft crackle of the record player remained. Yet Tom could still hear the overtones of his clarinet from earlier that evening.

Elaine turned to Tom. "Want to walk me home?"

He became hesitant, then smiled. "I'd like that."

They stepped outside into the hush of new snow. Tom locked the door behind him. Harmony Lane lay before them, glowing with string lights and lanterns. The night was full of possibility, wrapped in scarves and song. People were enjoying the sidewalk Christmas carolers to continue their time outdoors, making new friends and sharing time with ones they knew.

Tom offered her his arm, and she took it. As they walked in unhurried steps past shuttered shops and glowing windows, Elaine looked up at the sky. "I love that it's snowing," she whispered.

Tom glanced upward, then at her. "It's like the night doesn't want to end."

She let out a soft breath. "Do you ever feel like this whole town is wrapped in some kind of hopeful dream?"

Tom smiled. "Yeah. Tonight, it does feel that way. Like we all entered something rare."

A few houses twinkled in the distance, their holiday lights reflected in patches of ice along the sidewalk. The rhythm of their footsteps in the snow was still unhurried, peaceful between old friends finding their way to something new.

Elaine spoke again, almost to herself. "I used to think quiet meant lonely. But now it means room for something new."

He turned to her, being thoughtful. "And maybe it means being present enough to notice the things that matter."

She looked up at him, her expression softening was her response.

They said nothing for a few steps, letting the snow speak in soft hushes, and the distant bell of the clock tower rang its hour. Without sharing separately, they each continued to hear the music played from the shop.

And in that moment, the cold didn't matter, nor did the years or fears they'd carried. What mattered was this beginning. Quiet, courageous, and real.

A New Song for Two

CHRISTMAS DAY ARRIVED WITH a sense of calm and anticipation. Harmony Lane was gifted with a fresh coat of snow, light and powdery, sparkling beneath a pale sun. The town moved at a slower pace that morning. The usual bustle was replaced by the quiet rituals of the holiday in everyone's homes. Coffee brewing, carols playing, the rustle of wrapping paper, and the laughter of children carried through frost-glazed windows.

Elaine stood at the window of her cottage, cradling a mug of cinnamon tea in her hands. She wore the gifted scarf Tom gave back to her last night after his performance. He'd wrapped it around her neck and said, "Seems like it belongs with you after all."

The memory warmed her more than the tea. The exhibit had been a success in every sense. Her tapestries sparked conversations, invitations, and even a potential commission arrangement. But more than that, the evening had marked a shift. Quiet but unmistakable in her spirit. And also in Tom's.

She thought of his music, recalling the way he played not to impress, but to reconnect. Yet another something new opened between them at that moment. It lingered now, like a melody hanging with no last note.

She set her mug down and strolled through the cozy cottage, trailing her fingers along the backs of chairs and the windowsill where a sprig of holly leaned inside. It had been a long time since she'd felt like she belonged anywhere, even longer since she'd allowed herself to imagine anything new. Now, everything around her, the snow, the silence, even the warmth in her chest—whispered: stay.

On the mantel, she noticed the small ornament Tom had given her earlier in the week. A hand-carved bronze music note. It reminded her of an ornament she and Carol loved as kids that their parents would put on the tree each year. It was of an angel with a harp. She hadn't hung it yet. Now, as she walked over and nestled it on the small pine tree by the hearth, it felt symbolic. A pause finding its chord. A silence finding its voice. Like Tom's music, waiting to be heard.

Before she turned away, she added a few more touches to her little tree. A handful of ribbon scraps from her workshop, a painted bead from Morocco she'd been saving, and a tiny bell she found at the bottom of her sewing basket. Each item had its own story, and together, as they put decorations on the tree, they began a promise of newness. For the first time in years, she felt the ornaments weren't just memories, but part of her future in the making.

She paused, letting her eyes linger on the flickering firelight. She thought of past Christmases. Ones filled with empty chatter, airline terminals, or unfamiliar cities. Places she chose to be so she wouldn't feel the absence of what she no longer had. But here on Harmony Lane, the energy was different. Not hollow, but full. Full of meaning, full of presence.

A knock at the door stirred her from reflection. She opened it to find Tom, snowflakes clinging to his hair and shoulders, a warm grin softening his usual cautious features.

"Merry Christmas," he said, holding out a small paper bag. "From the cafe. Carol told me I should bring you something sweet. Although I had planned to do this anyway."

Elaine smiled and stepped aside. "Come in before you freeze."

Inside, the fire crackled. Tom handed her the bag. A cinnamon roll, still warm, as he glanced around.

"Cozy," he said. "And smells like pine and spice. You've made it a real home."

Elaine nodded. "It's growing on me. Like the snow. And the people who live here."

He looked at her for a moment, then cleared his throat. "I know it's Christmas and you might have plans, but... I was wondering if you'd like to come over and join me for some soup and music?"

Elaine tilted her head, amused. "Is that your version of a holiday feast?"

He chuckled. "That depends on whether you like homemade tomato soup and questionable Christmas playlists."

She smiled, her heart softening at his easy humor. "Sounds perfect."

They walked together to Tom's home, a short distance away. The snow muffled their steps, the lane still and bright. Along the way, neighbors waved from porches or called out holiday greetings, their voices carrying through the crisp air. Children bundled in scarves and boots played with sleds along a nearby hill, their laughter echoing against the white landscape. One little girl waved a mittened hand at

Elaine and shouted, "Merry Christmas, tapestry lady!" Elaine grinned and waved back, her heart full.

Tom's house was modest but filled with charm. Electric candles glowed in the windows, and the smell of tomatoes drifted from the kitchen. A small tree stood in the corner, its ornaments a mix of old glass balls and handmade treasures. Elaine paused before a clay angel with a chipped wing.

"An old friend made that," Tom mumbled. "Many years ago."

Elaine touched the angel. "It's beautiful."

Tom motioned for her to sit near the fire while he brought over two mugs of mulled cider with cloves and orange peel. Then, he brought over two bowls of his tomato soup. He handed her one and sat beside her.

They ate by the fire, mugs on the nearby table and bowls of soup in their laps, with the sound of a soft jazz record spinning in the background. Conversation came as they shared memories of awkward holiday dinners, favorite childhood gifts, and quiet reflections on years that had surprised them.

Elaine shared how she used to travel abroad during Christmas to escape the loneliness of being home alone. Booking art retreats in places like Lisbon and Kyoto just to stay distracted. Tom talked about volunteering at the community kitchen in town. Something he did every year as a way of helping others, because it was the one place where no one expected him to smile if he didn't feel like it.

Elaine leaned back with her cider and looked toward the fireplace. "Funny how grief used to make everything feel hollow. I'd move through the holidays like a ghost, checking off days. But here... it's like the season found its heartbeat again."

Tom stirred the fire with a small iron poker. "Harmony Lane has a way of doing that. It's not flashy, not loud. But it listens. It holds you in place long enough for something good to catch up."

"I never thought I'd enjoy Christmas again," Elaine said after a while. "It used to feel...empty. Like something lost. But this year, here, with you and all the others, it feels different. Like there's something to step into instead of away from."

Tom nodded. "I used to dread this day. The silence of it. But today, it feels more like a pause than an ache. Like life's giving us a moment to listen, to renew."

Elaine turned to him, her voice barely above a whisper. "What do you hear?"

He looked at her, searching, gentle. "Possibility."

Outside, snow began to fall again. Lazy, delicate flakes that were beautiful to watch as they drifted to the ground.

Tom stood and walked to the bookshelf. From behind a row of music biographies, he pulled out his clarinet case.

Elaine watched, her breath catching.

"I've been thinking," he said as he opened the case, "about second chances. About music, and... about us."

She said nothing, but her eyes held steady.

He lifted the clarinet, turning it in his hands. "Would you mind if I played something? Just for you?"

Elaine shook her head, her smile soft. "I'd love that."

He brought the instrument to his lips and began to play. Not a formal piece, but a delightful melody he'd composed over the last few weeks. It had no name, yet it was filled with emotion: gentle hope, tentative wonder, and the anticipation of something new taking root.

Elaine closed her eyes, letting the notes wrap around her like a shawl. It was enjoyable and sincere. Each note seemed to offer a question followed by an answer: Are you here? Yes. Are you ready? Almost. Do you believe? I'm trying.

When the ending note lingered and then stopped, Tom lowered his clarinet. Elaine opened her eyes, tears glistening, her smile steady.

She crossed the room and stood before him. "That was the most beautiful gift I've received in years."

Tom set the instrument aside. "I wasn't sure I could still play like that. Or feel like that."

Elaine took his hand. "You can. And you did."

They stood for a long moment, the fire crackling behind them, the snow still falling beyond the windows.

Elaine spoke. "I extended my stay."

Tom blinked. "You did?"

"The cottage is available through spring. And, well... I'm not quite ready to leave Harmony Lane."

A smile spread across Tom's face. "I'm glad."

Elaine squeezed his hand. "There's something about this place, about you, and this town. It feels like a new beginning I didn't know I needed."

Tom nodded. "Maybe we both needed it. Maybe everything before was just leading each of us to this."

He stepped closer. "So, what do we do with a beginning like that?"

Elaine looked up at him. "We take our time. We enjoy your soup and music. We walk in the snow. And when we're ready... we write the next part together."

He leaned in, pressing a gentle kiss on her forehead. "I'd like that."

Later that evening, they bundled up and walked outside again. The snow had deepened, soft and undisturbed. Elaine laughed as she reached down and scooped a handful, tossing it at Tom. He shielded his face and retaliated with a handful of his own, the two of them ducking and dancing in a flurry of joy.

After that moment, they paused, breathless and flushed. Tom gazed at her, something tender flickering behind his eyes. "I think I've laughed more this month than I have in years."

Elaine reached for his hand. "Then we're doing something right."

They continued their walk, meandering past Christmas-lit windows and snow-dusted rooftops. From one house, a carol floated into the night. "O Holy Night" played on an old upright piano. Elaine stopped to listen.

"I always loved this song," she said. "There's something so still and reverent about it. Like the world pauses to listen."

Tom nodded. "It reminds me of my father. He used to play it every year, no matter what kind of day we were having."

The melody lingered as they stood together, the silence between them full of shared memories and newfound peace.

Back at Tom's house, they lit more candles and made tea, curling up on the couch under a quilt stitched decades ago by Tom's mother. They spoke in whispers, sharing old dreams they once tucked away.

Elaine revealed a scrapbook she kept of all the places she wanted to visit but never had. Tom promised they'd start a new one come spring. They even made a playful list of ideas, such as stargazing in Bryce Canyon, taking a cooking class in New Orleans, learning to waltz just for fun. It was the kind of list you made when life felt possible again.

Before she left that night, he pressed a wrapped package into her hands. Something small and square. She opened it to find a framed copy of a musical score titled *"A New Song for Two."* The notation was his own.

Elaine looked up, eyes wide. "You wrote this?"

He nodded. "I wanted you to have it. For all the new beginnings neither of us saw coming."

They stood in silence for a long beat, then moved to the window. Snowfall dusted the town in moonlight and a soft and luminous hush. Tom reached for her hand again, and they stood there, soaking in the quiet together.

Elaine whispered, "Maybe we don't have to know where it's going. Maybe it's enough to begin."

Tom nodded, eyes never leaving hers. "As long as we begin together."

In that moment, the fireplace dimmed. The night folded around them, and they stood as two people no longer defined by their endings, but by the hope and harmony of something just beginning.

Outside the town felt new. Inside, their song was beginning to be played.

The End

Have a look at my book Christmas by the Lake

If you enjoyed *Christmas on Harmony Lane*, you may also love spending the holidays at the lake.

On the quiet lakeshore of a small Midwestern town, Christmas lights shimmer on the water. Old memories stir, and two people who never expected a second chance find themselves drawn together by shared hurts, gentle laughter, and the courage to hope again.

It's a tender story of healing, new beginnings, and the spirit of Christmas that changes the way you see the future.

If you're ready for another cozy holiday escape, dive into the world of *Christmas by the Lake*.

Other Books by Drew Beyson

innercouncilpublications.com

Check out My Moon View Series Prequel - Free Book

Check Out My Moon View Series Prequel — Free Book

As a thank you for reading, I offer a special prequel to the Moon View Series; A warm, heartfelt introduction that captures the moment when everything begins.

To download your free copy, scan the QR code below or go to https://BookHip.com/JDGRDKW or visit link below:

InnerCouncilPublications.com

This story is my gift to you. I hope you enjoy your visit to Moon View.

About Author

Drew Beyson writes heartwarming clean romance filled with gentle emotion, hopeful new beginnings, and the quiet magic tucked into everyday life. Her stories invite readers into cozy settings, tender connections, and moments of healing that remind us all that love can bloom in the most unexpected places.

When she isn't writing, Drew enjoys savoring a warm cup of tea or hot chocolate, baking cookies, and taking peaceful strolls in nature. Her time in nature often inspires her stories, characters, and scenes. She treasures the comfort of cozy moments, heartfelt conversations, and the beauty found in slowing down.

To learn more about Drew's books, visit:
innercouncilpublications.com

www.ingramcontent.com/pod-product-compliance
Lightning Source LLC
Chambersburg PA
CBHW020313150626
46552CB00022B/2864